SOPHIE
SHYOSAURUS

First edition for the United States published in 2014 by Barron's Educational Series, Inc.

First published in 2013 by Wayland

Text copyright © Brian Moses
Illustrations © Mike Gordon

Wayland
338 Euston Road, London, NW13BH
Wayland is a division of Hachette Children's Books, a Hachette U.K. company

The right of Brian Moses to be identified as the author and Mike Gordon as the illustrator of the Work has been asserted by them in accordance with the Copyright, Designs and Patent Act 1988.

All inquiries should be addressed to:
Barron's Educational Series, Inc.
250 Wireless Boulevard
Hauppauge, NY 11788
www.barronseduc.com

ISBN: 978-1-4380-0406-8

Library of Congress Control Number:
  2013939931

Date of Manufacture: December 2013
Manufactured by: WKT Company Ltd.,
  Shenzhen, Guangdong, China

Product conforms to all applicable CPSC and CPSIA 2008 standards. No lead or phthalate hazard.

Printed in China
9 8 7 6 5 4 3 2 1

SOPHIE SHYOSAURUS

Written by
Brian Moses

Illustrated by
Mike Gordon

Can you see
Sophie Shyosaurus?

4

Sophie really is
very shy and quite often,
when visitors call, she
hides away.

But maybe you
can spot her?

Sophie doesn't like meeting adult dinosaurs. She blushes and gets tongue-tied.

She never knows what to say.

Sophie wants to go to parties, but she isn't happy being with dinosaurs she doesn't know.

She asks her Mom to stay with her until
she finds someone she can play with.

Sophie feels shy when she's asked
to talk in front of her class at school.
Her mouth goes dry and she
can't think of what to say.

Sometimes she starts to cry.

Sophie's Mom and Dad are always
telling her not to worry about it.

"It's okay to feel shy," her Dad tells her. "Everyone feels shy at some time or other."

"When I first met the manager at Beastly Towers, the hotel where I work," Sophie's Dad explained, "I just didn't know what to say."

"And when I did say something, the words were wrong. That was all because I felt a bit shy."

15

"But I don't like feeling shy," Sophie said. "I love to dance, but if I know someone is watching, I feel embarrassed and I have to stop."

"Will I ever stop feeling shy?"
Sophie wondered.

"Let's see if we can help you," her Dad said. "When you meet other dinosaurs, there's no need to hide away. Let's practice what you might say."

"Sometimes it helps to do something for someone, and to smile at them when you offer."

Can I help you carry your bags?

"That someone you help may
even become a new friend."

"Sometimes taking a special toy to
school can help when you're feeling shy.
You can cuddle your toy, or maybe someone
else will have the same toy and you
can play together."

"Very soon other dinosaurs
may want to play with you as well."

"Everyone has something
they're good at,"
Sophie's Mom said.
"You're good at dancing."

"But if you feel shy when other dinosaurs are watching you, it's just because they like your dancing," her Dad said. "They might even join in, too."

Sophie is still a little bit shy, but she's working hard every day at leaving her shyness behind.

And the other
day she even
won a medal
for her dancing.

NOTES FOR PARENTS AND TEACHERS

Read the book with children either individually or in groups.
Talk to them about what makes someone shy. How do
children feel when they are shy?

How would they picture that shyness? Would it feel like having
butterflies in your tummy, or being red faced, or wanting to be invisible?

Help children compose short poems about the times that they feel shy.

       I feel shy when I'm with children I haven't met before.
       I feel shy when I'm asked to talk in front of my class.
       I feel shy when everyone's watching me.
       I feel shy...

Talk to children about how they behave when they feel shy
and write down their ideas so they can be discussed.

       Days when I'm shy, I just want to hide.
       I want to be invisible, in a place where no one sees me.
       I want to be behind the couch, in another room.
       Just let me roll up into a ball and pretend I'm not here.

Remind them that shyness is a feeling, and like other feelings, it can
come and go. Can they think of situations in which they don't feel
shy? Perhaps when they are with friends and family. Perhaps when
they are doing something they are good at.

Think about situations where children might feel shy and use them for role play. One child might play the part of an adult meeting a child for the first time. Help children write down what they might say on pieces of card and then practice saying the lines.

If a child has to give a talk at school, help him or her write out the talk first and practice saying it in front of the mirror. The more the lines are read aloud, the more confident children will get about saying them in front of others.

Can children find other words for "shy"—timid, nervous, cautious, bashful? One of the dwarfs in the story of *Snow White* was called Bashful. Children might enjoy watching the film and looking out for him.

Always be positive when discussing shyness. Remind children that everyone is good at something and that confidence in this area can help children lose their shyness.

Explore the notion of shyness further through the sharing of picture books mentioned in the book list on page 32.

BOOKS TO SHARE

Are You Shy?   Jennifer Moore-Mallinos
Explores how children can learn to speak up and overcome shyness little by little.

It's OK to Be Me!   Jennifer Moore-Mallinos
The boy in this story is in a wheelchair, but he doesn't let that stop him from joining the basketball team!

Sometimes I Feel...Sunny   Gillian Shields,
Illustrated by Georgie Birkett
Explores the emotions that kids go through, from being sunny and brave to feeling small and sad.

I Can Do It!: A First Look at Not Giving Up   Pat Thomas
Learning new things—even when they are scary or difficult—makes life more interesting.

Why Do I Feel Scared?: A First Look at Being Brave   Pat Thomas
There are lots of ways to be brave. This book explores them, and lets kids know that it's okay to feel scared.